DEINONYCHUS

PROTOCERATOPS

LAMBEOSAURUS

POLACANTHUS

AMARGASAURUS

CRYOLOPHOSAURUS

GORGOSAURUS

SPINOSAURUS

SUPERSAURUS

QUETZALCOATLUS

To wee David, who is a splendid dinosaur
J. Y.
For Michael Cavanaugh
M. T.

HarperCollins *Children's Books*

First published in hardback by Scholastic Inc., USA in 2005
First published in paperback in Great Britain by HarperCollins Children's Books in 2006

3 5 7 9 10 8 6 4 2
ISBN 978-0-00-780025-4
Text copyright © Jane Yolen 2005
Illustrations copyright © Mark Teague 2005
All rights reserved. Published by arrangement with Scholastic Inc., 557 Broadway, New York, NY 10012, USA.
The author and illustrator assert the moral right to be identified as the author and illustrator of the work.
No part of this publication may be reproduced without the prior permission of
HarperCollins Publishers Ltd, 77-85 Fulham Palace Road, Hammersmith, London W6 8JB.
Visit our website at: www.harpercollins.co.uk
Printed in China by South China Printing Co. Ltd.

Other titles in the series:

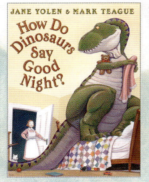

ISBN: 0-00-713728-1

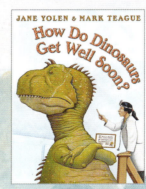

ISBN: 0-00-717236-2

JANE YOLEN

How Do Dinosaurs Eat Their Food?

Illustrated by

MARK TEAGUE

How does a dinosaur
eat all his food?
Does he burp,
does he belch,
or make noises
quite rude?

Does he pick at his cereal,

throw down

his cup,

hoping to make

someone else

pick it up?

Does he fuss, does he fidget,
or squirm in his chair?

Does he flip his spaghetti

high into the air?

SUPERSAURUS

DOES

A DINOSAUR

GLARE?

How does a dinosaur
eat all his food?
Does he spit
out his broccoli
partially chewed?

SPINOSAURUS

Does he bubble

his milk?

Stick beans

up his nose?

GORGOSAURUS

Does he squeeze juicy oranges

with his big toes?

POLACANTHUS

No . . .

He says, "Please"

and "Thank you."
He sits very still.

He eats all before him
with smiles and goodwill.

He tries

every new thing,

at least one

small bite.

He makes

no loud noises –

that isn't polite.

He never
drops anything
on to the floor.
And after
he's finished,
he asks for
some more.

Eat up.

Eat up, little dinosaur.